WINGMAKER

For my nephew James — D.C.

For my 77-year-old mother, whose quilting and curiosity
inspire me to keep reinventing my art — D.H.

Published in Canada and the U.S. by Kids Can Press Ltd.
25 Dockside Drive, Toronto, ON M5A 0B5

Kids Can Press is a Corus Entertainment Inc. company

www.kidscanpress.com

The artwork in this book was rendered in pixels, with imaginary pencils,
digital smudges and a handful of colors picked from an infinite palette.
The text is set in ITC Tiepolo.

Edited by Jennifer Stokes
Designed by Marie Bartholomew

Printed and bound in Buji, Shenzhen, China in 10/2020 by WKT Company

CM 21 0 9 8 7 6 5 4 3 2 1

Library and Archives Canada Cataloguing in Publication

Title: Wingmaker / written by Dave Cameron ; illustrated by David Huyck.
Names: Cameron, Dave, 1974— author. | Huyck, David, 1976— illustrator.
Identifiers: Canadiana 20200231944 | ISBN 9781525302374 (hardcover)
Classification: LCC PS8605.A48115 W56 2021 | DDC jC813/.6—dc23

Kids Can Press gratefully acknowledges that the land on which our
office is located is the traditional territory of many nations, including
the Mississaugas of the Credit, the Anishnabeg, the Chippewa, the
Haudenosaunee and the Wendat peoples, and is now home to many
diverse First Nations, Inuit and Métis peoples.

We thank the Government of Ontario, through Ontario Creates;
the Ontario Arts Council; the Canada Council for the Arts; and the
Government of Canada for supporting our publishing activity.

WINGMAKER

Dave Cameron

David Huyck

Kids Can Press

Leaf and Lou lived in a colony at the foot of a tall cherry tree.

They spent their days caring for the queen and the larvae, finding food and keeping the tunnels of their busy anthill clean and tidy.

After a long day of work, Leaf and Lou often traveled up the tree and to the end of a branch to visit an old, old caterpillar whom everyone called Gramma Tinker.

Gramma was an inventor, and she loved to build simple tools to help her friends. For Leaf, she'd invented scissors for faster leaf-cutting. And for Lou, she'd designed a handy wagon that carried many grains of sand all at once.

But Gramma's most famous invention was a fourteen-pedal bicycle. Every caterpillar in the forest wanted one!

One day, Leaf and Lou arrived at the end of the branch to find Gramma Tinker creating something large and billowy.

"Is this your latest invention?" Leaf asked.

"It's my greatest invention yet!" said Gramma. "It's woven of the strongest silk. I call it the Wingmaker 77 because that's how old I am!"

"You're 77?" asked Leaf.

"Years old?" asked Lou.

Gramma laughed. "I'm 77 *days* old!" she said.

"Who is the Wingmaker for?" asked Leaf, helping Gramma down from her loom.

"It's for me," Gramma said. "Custom made!"

"Why do you need to make wings?" asked Lou, busily fluffing pillows.

"Good question," said Gramma, as she crawled stiffly on to her lounger. Each time Leaf and Lou saw her, she was using more canes and moving more and more slowly. "All I know for sure is that I'm preparing for a new adventure."

Gramma yawned. "When the Wingmaker is finished, I'll rest inside it for two weeks. When I wake up, I'll be changed."

"Two weeks!" Leaf said. He thought that seemed like a long time to be asleep. "Why will you change?"

"Because my time has come," Gramma said.

"*How* will you change?" Lou asked.

"That's the magical part. For all the books I've read, I still can't get my mind around it." The old caterpillar yawned again. "Come back tomorrow. Some special guests are dropping by to help me figure it out."

Leaf and Lou didn't go home right away.
Worried that Gramma Tinker was so busy
with her Wingmaker that she wasn't eating
enough, they spent part of the night cutting
leaves and piling them at her door.

And they couldn't stop talking about her
new adventure and her special guests.

When they arrived the next day, Gramma Tinker was at her desk. A fly whizzed into the workshop and buzzed around her head.

"Fly, be still!" she said. "I need to study your wings."

The insect landed, and the buzzing stopped.

Gramma gently lifted one of its wings. "It weighs nothing at all," she said, amazed.

"If my wings were heavy, I'd be stuck on the ground," the fly said. "I'd be a creepy-crawly thing."

The fly looked at the caterpillar and the two ants. "No offense," it said, then zipped out the window.

WEIGHT
WINGSPAN

Soon after, a hummingbird flitted through the window and darted here, there and everywhere.

"You're a windy one!" Gramma said. She put on a hat and scarf. Then she offered the bird some sugar water so that it might stay in one place. The hummingbird hovered and drank.

"Why do you flutter so fast?" Gramma asked.

"Speedy wings let me move in any direction — up, down, sideways — or in no direction at all," the hummingbird said. "Gotta go!"

And off it went.

As it grew dark outside, a bat came and hung upside down from the window sash.

"Taking off takes some practice, and landing can be a trick," the bat said.

It flew away, did a couple of loop the loops and returned to the window.

"Incredible!" Gramma said.

"Easier than it looks," the bat said. "You'll find a method that works for you."

"The Moth Method!" Gramma said.

After the bat disappeared into the dusk, Gramma Tinker realized how late it was. "You should get home, my little friends. I still have work to do."

"Are you going on your adventure now?" asked Leaf.

"Soon," said Gramma.

"What did you mean by the Moth Method?" asked Lou.

"You'll see," said Gramma Tinker. "There's something I'll need your help with. Come back in two weeks."

In the days that followed, Leaf and Lou worked hard. Leaf was put in charge of feeding the larvae, and Lou was asked to take out the colony's garbage. Every so often, the two ants would stop working, look up at Gramma Tinker's branch and wonder.

When the two weeks had finally passed, Leaf and Lou returned to the end of the branch. Gramma's workshop was empty and quiet, and there was a letter waiting for them.

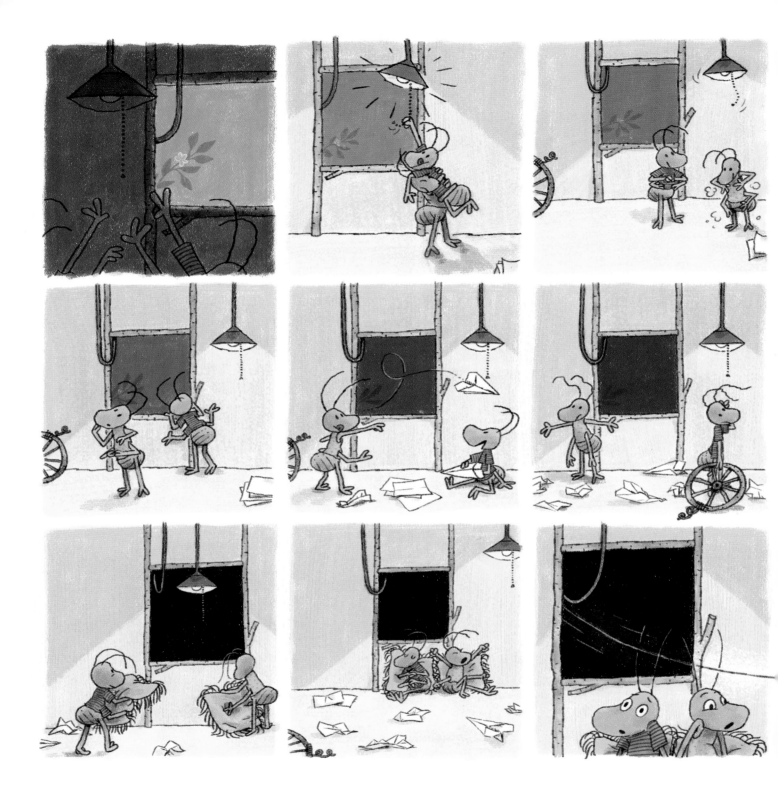

Leaf and Lou pulled the lamp chain. In the bright workshop, they waited and waited. The room seemed to get brighter as day became night.

All of a sudden, a moth dipped into the room
and began circling the light bulb.
    Leaf and Lou sat up and stared.
    "Is it her?" Leaf whispered to Lou.
    "Is it you?" Lou asked the moth.

"Yes. I'm still me!" Gramma Tinker said.
"My Wingmaker worked its magic, and
now I'm setting off on my new adventure!"

Gramma circled
the bulb once more,
and Leaf and Lou
watched in wonder
as she flew off into
the night.

About Gramma Tinker

Gramma Tinker is an eastern tent caterpillar, native to North America. Colorful and highly social, these caterpillars undergo a complete transformation known as metamorphosis [met-uh-MOR-fuh-sis]. After hatching from its egg in early spring, the caterpillar forages, or looks for food, for approximately two months — 77 days, in Gramma Tinker's case. It then looks for somewhere to make a cocoon, a silky case that protects the caterpillar during what is called the pupa stage [PYOO-puh]. Two weeks later, it emerges as a lappet moth.

A female lappet moth like Gramma Tinker has a wingspan of about 5 cm (2 in.). It feeds on leaves and shrubs and pollinates flowers that are open at night.

While the eastern tent caterpillar is diurnal, or most active in the daytime, the lappet moth it becomes is nocturnal, or active only at night. Lappet moths are positively phototactic [foh-toh-TAK-tik], which means they're automatically drawn to sources of light.

Turn on your porch light tonight and see how many moths come to visit you!